DEPOMPA

From his home on the other side of the moon, Father Time summoned his most trusted storytellers to bring a message of hope to all children. Their mission was to spread magical tales throughout the world: tales that remind us that we all belong to one family, one world; that our hearts speak the same language, no matter where we live or how different we look or sound; and that we each have the right to be loved, to be nurtured, and to reach for a dream.

This is one of their stories.
Listen with your heart and share the magic.

For Sylvie and
her uncle Rick,
whose capacity
to love continues
to awaken
our hearts.

Special thanks to the talented artists who contributed their time and faith to these pages; to our Cedco Publishing champions Charles Ditlefsen, Mary Sullivan, Deborah Kamradt and Susan Ristow; and to the team of believers at Portofino Art Management, whose supreme dedication made this book possible, we offer our heartfelt applause.

The Little Snow Bear

An Original American Tale

Flavia and Lisa Weedn

Illustrated by Flavia Weedn

Cedco Publishing Company • San Rafael, California

Once upon a time, in a village near a
great forest, there lived a little bear.

Although there were other bears who lived nearby in the village, they were all much older and much bigger.

No matter how hard he tried, he could never run as fast or jump as high as they could. And no matter how much he pretended to be as big as they were, he was still just a little bear.

Because of this, the little bear was very sad and lonely, and more than anything he wished for a friend to be with—someone just like him.

One winter day he saw the other bears playing in the snow. They were making snowpeople. The little bear knew he couldn't make snowpeople as big as the others could. But maybe he could make a little bear out of snow—a little bear just like him—and maybe this little snow bear could be his friend.

So late that night, in his backyard where no one could see him, he began.

The little bear worked and worked, and by early morning he was finished. He had made a wonderful snow bear that looked just like him. At last he had a friend of his very own.

The little bear gave his friend a coat, a
scarf, and boots, and they played together in
the snow all day until it got dark.

"Remember now," said the snow bear to the little
bear, "I am made out of snow, so I must sleep outside in
the cold."

The little bear understood this and was so happy to have
a friend that he made a bed for the snow bear just outside
his own bedroom window.

All through the night, whenever the little bear would awake, he would peek through the window to see the snow bear. He was afraid it was all a dream, but it wasn't, for the snow bear was always there.

Every day the two little friends would play together. Sometimes they would read books to each other, play games in the snow, or fly the little bear's kite.

And every night the little bear would go inside his house to sleep while the snow bear would sleep just outside his window.

What they liked to do best was to lie outside
on the little bear's favorite quilt and look up at the night sky.
They would watch the stars and the moon, and they would
wonder about the world.

It was the best winter the little bear had ever known,
and he never felt lonely, not even once. He was so very,
very happy.

Then one night the snow bear had something important to tell the little bear. "Tomorrow," he said, "is the first day of spring, so I will have to go away. I am made of snow, so I must follow the winter and the frost."

The little bear cried and cried and said, "Oh, please don't leave me. You are my best friend, my only friend."

The snow bear took the little bear's hand and answered softly, "But I will come back when the winter comes again, and we will play together just like we do now, I promise."

The next morning the little bear looked out the window and saw that the snow bear had melted away. There beside the bed the little bear had made for him were the snow bear's scarf, coat, and boots— but the snow bear was gone.

Then the little bear noticed that something was inside one of the boots. It was a note from the snow bear.

It read: "It is true, I am your friend, but I am not your only friend. After I have gone, you will realize you have other friends, and you will discover a brand-new friend, a friend called 'remembering.'"

The little bear was still sad, but all through that day and the next few days he kept thinking about the snow bear and how much he missed him. Then he began to think about all the wonderful things they had done together.

He remembered how they had read books
and pretended, and how they had tried to sing
songs with the snowbirds. He remembered how they
had laughed when they had flown his kite and how they
had watched the moon and stars in the night sky, and
how they had shared the wonder of the world together.

In his heart he remembered everything. Then he began to realize he still had all these things. The snowbirds were still there. They were his friends. His kite was still there, and it was his friend. And the moon and stars, they were his friends, too. They were still up in the sky just like they had been before.

The snow bear had been right—the little bear did have other friends. And now the little bear understood what the snow bear's note meant about discovering that "remembering" was a friend, too.

By remembering the snow bear, the little bear was keeping his friend close to him. It was almost like doing all the things they had done together all over again—and this made the little bear feel good inside.

All through the year the little bear could hardly wait for the winter to come again so that he could tell the snow bear the wonderful things he had discovered about friendship and the magic of remembering.

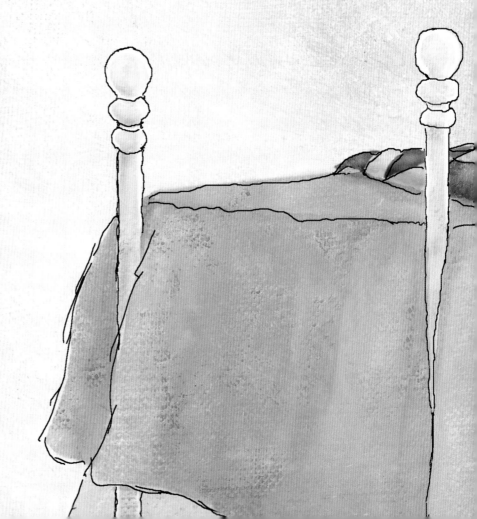

And then, finally, the winter came and with it came the little snow bear, just as he had promised. And for every winter after that, the two little friends were always together.

The little bear was never lonely again, for he was too busy making memories, memories he would keep forever, with his special friend made out of snow.

ISBN 0-7683-2055-0

Text by Flavia and Lisa Weedn
Illustrations by Flavia Weedn
© Weedn Family Trust
www.flavia.com

Published in 1998 by Cedco Publishing Company.
100 Pelican Way, San Rafael, California 94901
For a free catalog of other Cedco® products, please write
to the address above, or visit our website: www.cedco.com

Printed in Hong Kong

The artwork for each picture is
digitally mastered using acrylic on canvas.
This book is set in Journal Text.